Jasper John Dooley

You're in Trouble

Jasper John Dooley

You're in Trouble

Written by Caroline Adderson
Illustrated by Ben Clanton

Kids Can Press

For my sister, who was never, ever bad — C.A.

Kids Can Press acknowledges the financial support of the Government of Ontario, through the Ontario Media Development Corporation's Ontario Book Initiative; the Ontario Arts Council; the Canada Council for the Arts; and the Government of Canada, through the CBF, for our publishing activity.

Published in Canada by
Kids Can Press Ltd.
25 Dockside Drive
Toronto, ON M5A 0B5

Published in the U.S. by
Kids Can Press Ltd.
2250 Military Road
Tonawanda, NY 14150

www.kidscanpress.com

Edited by Yasemin Uçar
Series designed by Marie Bartholomew
Designed by Julia Naimska

This book is smyth sewn casebound.
Manufactured in Shen Zhen, Guang Dong, P.R. China, in 10/2014 by Printplus Limited

CM 15 0 9 8 7 6 5 4 3 2 1

Library and Archives Canada Cataloguing in Publication

Adderson, Caroline, author
Jasper John Dooley you're in trouble / written by Caroline Adderson ; illustrated by Ben Clanton.

(Jasper John Dooley ; 4)
ISBN 978-1-55453-808-9 (bound)

I. Clanton, Ben, 1988–, illustrator II. Title.
III. Series: Adderson, Caroline, Jasper John Dooley ; 4

PS8551.D3267J37 2014 jC813'.54 C2014-902852-0

Kids Can Press is a Corus™ Entertainment company

Contents

Chapter 1

After soccer practice, Jasper John Dooley's dad gave him change to buy a drink. "You must be really thirsty after all that running away from the ball," he said.

"It's because of my striped socks," Jasper told him.

"I'm just going to ask Coach Ben a quick question. You go ahead."

Jasper took the change and skipped away. Dad waited in the parking lot beside Coach Ben's car. Dad's question was going to be quick for sure. It only had three letters — W-H-Y? During practice, Dad had stood on the sidelines shaking his head and asking the other parents the same thing. "Why?"

Why does Jasper always run *away* from the ball? he meant.

Why do bees have stripes? Jasper wondered, but as soon as he reached the vending machines, he stopped thinking about bees.

Two machines stood in front of the community center, one for candy and chips, the other for drinks. Jasper spent a few minutes looking in the candy and chip machine. He liked how the things were arranged inside, with the chips in the top three rows and the chocolate bars in the middle two rows. In the bottom row were the not-chip and not-chocolate bar things, the things that didn't fit, like cookies and gummies.

Jasper leaned right into the machine so that his breath clouded over the glass. If only he had more money! He looked at the change Dad had given him, but didn't count it, because that would be math. Anyway, he could tell there wasn't enough for a drink *and* chips, or a drink *and* a chocolate bar, or a drink *and* gummies.

He checked the coin returns. He got down on his hands and his knees and looked under the machines. Nobody had accidentally left change behind, or dropped it, so he could buy a drink *and* something else.

Then he remembered Dad was only asking a quick question and moved over to the drink machine.

There were two kinds of drinks — good and bad. The good drinks had happy face stickers on their labels. The bad ones didn't. They were full of things that were bad for you, like sugar. Jasper was only allowed bad things full of sugar as a special treat and only after he had eaten good things. Like celery. He might be allowed a bad drink if he ate some celery first. But he hadn't eaten celery for a long, long time. He hated it.

So he had to choose a good drink — apple juice or water. Water! Who would buy water? The water in the drinking fountain was free.

Jasper got an idea. He'd go into the community center and drink some water from the fountain. That way he would have enough money for a drink *and* chips, or a drink *and* a chocolate bar, or a drink *and* gummies.

In the parking lot, Dad was talking to Coach Ben. Coach Ben was patting him on the shoulder like he was almost finished answering his question. If they finished talking while Jasper was inside getting a free drink, when Dad came to meet him at the vending machines, Jasper wouldn't be there. Then the thing that had happened in the grocery store a long time ago would happen again. Dad would run around yelling and waving his arms. The loudspeaker would boom out, "Code Red! Code Red!" Jasper would drop whatever was in his hand — change today, or a whole carton of blueberries in the grocery store — because he was so frightened.

Apple juice, Jasper decided.

His money clattered down. Words started scrolling by on the little screen above the coin slot. YOUR SELECTION NOW PLEASE PRESS YOUR SELECTION NOW PLEASE ... *Beep!*

Each of the cans and bottles had a letter and a number. The letter and number for apple juice was *C3*.

PRESS YOUR SELECTION NOW PLEASE PRESS YOUR SELECTION ... *Beep!*

NOW PLEASE PRESS YOUR ... *Beep! Beep! BEEP!*

Hurry! Hurry! Jasper pressed *C* on the keypad, then 3.

Scary noises — whirrs and rumbles and clanks — started up. The whole machine shook with these sounds. A can shot forward, held by the machine's claws. The machine seemed to be showing Jasper the can — it was red and black with a picture of a torpedo on it. When the claws let go, the can crashed to the bottom of the machine and rolled out of view.

Jasper squatted. He was almost afraid to push against the door and see the drink waiting there. Because apple juice came in bottles, not cans. Also, he was pretty sure that apple juice would have a happy face, not a torpedo.

He reached inside and took out the can — the can of Torpedo High Energy Drink.

He pressed it to his cheek. Cold.

Cold, and so so Bad.

In the parking lot, Coach Ben was loading a big net bag of soccer balls into the trunk of his car. Dad was still asking, "Why?"

Dad might not let Jasper drink the Bad drink even though he'd already bought it. But if Jasper opened it and started drinking now, he would at least get to taste some of the Bad drink before he had to pour it out.

He stepped around the side of the machine where Dad wouldn't see him and pulled the tab.

First came the sound of a torpedo firing. Fizzy brown liquid bubbled out and over his hand. Jasper leaned away from the can. When he was sure it wouldn't explode, he changed hands and licked the sweet drink off his fingers. His tongue prickled like there were tiny bombs going off in his mouth.

"Wow!" he said.

"Jasper!" Dad shouted, making Jasper swing around and splash Bad drink onto Dad's pants. Jasper shrank down. He looked from the can to Dad's pants, then up to his face.

Dad said, "You scared me! I looked over and you weren't here!"

He was breathing hard from running all the way from the parking lot. He didn't seem to notice the Bad drink splash on his pants. "Come here, Jasper," he said, grabbing him and hugging so hard that some of the Bad drink spurted out of the can like water in a fountain. It spurted up the back of Dad's jacket.

"Phew!" he said.

On the way to the car, Dad squeezed and unsqueezed Jasper's shoulder. "Remember that time? You were about three, I guess. I lost you in the grocery store …"

"Yes!" Jasper said, holding the Bad drink out so he wouldn't get splashed, too, while Dad squeezed him. "I do remember."

"It was horrible. I felt like that just now."

And Dad squeezed him even harder.

Chapter 2

Before they got in the car, Jasper showed Dad the Torpedo High Energy Drink. He said, "Look what came out of the machine. I wanted apple juice."

Dad wasn't focusing, Jasper could tell. Usually Dad passed the key toggle to Jasper so he could unlock the car and make it beep. It was a nice beep, not an impatient beep like the drink machine had made. The beep of the car meant, "Hello! Where would you like to go?" The drink machine beep meant, "Hurry! Hurry!"

Dad blinked at the red and black can in Jasper's hand.

"Can I drink it?" Jasper asked.

"You're thirsty, aren't you?"

Jasper took a so small sip. Right away his mouth exploded in prickles. When he swallowed, the prickles went down, too. But the drink was sweet, and as soon as he took one sip, he wanted another. He paused to scratch his tongue.

"Don't mention this to Mom, Jasper. Okay?"

The can was halfway to his mouth again. "The drink?" he asked.

"No. Don't say that I told you to go ahead and almost lost you. That other time? You were probably too young to notice, but she wouldn't speak to me for a whole week."

He opened the car door for Jasper. When he

turned to get in the car himself, Jasper saw the Bad drink stain on the back of Dad's jacket.

"Okay, Jasper John? We won't say anything, right?"

"Right," Jasper said just before he took a second sip.

This time it was a bigger sip. He had to shake his head around like he was doing the Hokey Pokey. He felt dizzy getting into the car. With the can between his knees, he fastened his seat belt — fast. Without a seat belt, he might blast right through the roof.

After that, for the whole drive home, Dad talked about soccer. He said, "Coach Ben thinks you're afraid of the ball. Are you afraid of the ball, Jasper?"

"Why would I be afraid of a ball?" Jasper asked, taking another tiny sip of the Torpedo High Energy Drink, then clenching his jaws so his head wouldn't blow off.

"Sometimes the ball comes at you pretty fast," Dad said. "I can see why you'd be afraid of it."

"But I'm not afraid of it," Jasper said. "I like fast things. I like so so fast things. I like things like torpedoes."

"Torpedoes?" Dad said, and Jasper giggled. His head felt like a balloon. It probably felt that way because of the enormous burp building up inside him.

BUUURRRPPP!!!

"Pardon me?" Dad said.

"That wasn't me," Jasper said. "That was the drink."

Dad laughed.

When they got home Jasper still hadn't finished the drink. He was afraid to because, after only five sips, the prickling had traveled all the way to his hands and feet. His head felt so floaty, but when he pressed it with his hands, it was still hard on the outside. Sixteen burps came out on the drive home.

"I'm not finished my drink," he told Dad as they got out of the car.

"Put it in the fridge," Dad said.

"Really?" Jasper said and, without waiting for an answer, he ran all the way into the house, trying not to spill any. He would spill less if he walked, but he found he couldn't walk. He only had one speed now. Fast!

The fridge was full. Any time there were leftovers, Jasper's mom put them in an empty yogurt container. When the fridge was full of yogurt containers, she started taking them out again and checking for food with green fur. Green fur meant the food got thrown out. Any food that wasn't furry went back in the fridge until it was.

There was just enough room at the back of the fridge for Jasper to tuck in the can of Torpedo High Energy Drink. He closed the door and took off running through the house.

"David?" Mom asked Dad. "What's that on your pants?"

Dad looked down at the Bad drink stain. "I have no idea."

Jasper ran right past them. Fast!

"Jasper John," Mom said, "didn't you use up any energy at soccer practice?"

"I used up some," Jasper called back. "Then I got a lot, lot more."

Chapter 3

During supper, Jasper kept bouncing on his chair because of his High Energy. When Mom and Dad asked him why he was bouncing, he said it helped his chewing.

After supper, his energy was still too high. Mom said, "Jasper John, it's not good to run and jump right after you've eaten."

Dad said, "Mom's right. Do you see what I do every day after supper? I lie on the sofa and watch golf on TV. It's the best thing for your digestion."

Mom said, "I feel dizzy just watching you, Jasper."

Jasper stopped running. "That's funny. Because I feel dizzy, too!"

Mom said riding a bike would be better, because his stomach wouldn't bounce around so much.

They went out to the alley together. Mom stood at one end watching for cars while Jasper rode up and down. Fast! He rode up and down so fast he made wind. A squirrel was sitting on the roof of the garage watching Jasper with wide eyes. Jasper's High Energy scared the squirrel. It ran up a telephone pole and away along the wire.

Jasper's friend Ori, who lived across the alley and one house down from Jasper, looked over the fence. "Do you want to ride bikes with me, Ori?" Jasper called as he zoomed past.

"The thing is, no," Ori said. "You're going too fast."

"Slow down, Jasper!" Mom called. "Stop!"

Jasper squeezed his brakes so they screeched like an angry cat. Mom had to jump out of the way.

"Look!" Ori said, pointing at the ground.

Jasper got off his bike and came over. His tires had made a long black skid mark. He squatted and touched the mark. It felt hot. He put his nose close and sniffed it.

Smoky.

Jasper remembered an expression his Nan used. "That's a black mark against him." It meant somebody had done a bad thing. She usually said it while watching the news on TV. Jasper had never wondered where the black mark got written down.

He didn't know it could be in the alley behind your house where everybody could see it.

"That's Bad," Ori said.

And Jasper said, "Wow!"

Before bed, Jasper took a bath. While he was in the tub, a tidal wave rose up and sank all his plastic boats.

Jasper wailed. Dad came running.

"Jasper, if you keep moving your legs like that, the seas get stormy."

"I can't help it," Jasper said.

"It's almost time to get out. Wash your hair, okay?"

Dad left. Jasper grabbed the shampoo and squeezed the bottle. His whole hand filled with blue goop. When he scrubbed, so so many suds formed that he could sculpt his hair into horns.

Jasper stood up in the tub so he could see himself in the mirror above the sink. "Ahh!" he cried. He looked so so so Bad!

Mom and Dad said "Ahh!" too, a minute later, when Jasper crept bare-naked into the living room and jumped out at them with a terrible roar. Mom actually screamed. Then she said he was dripping water and suds everywhere and he'd better march himself right back into the tub.

"Rinse that shampoo off and get ready for bed," she said. "Honestly, I don't know what's the matter with you tonight, Jasper John."

By the time Jasper got into bed he felt so so so tired from running away from the ball at soccer, from running and jumping in the house, and from riding his bike up and down the alley scaring squirrels and Ori and Mom. Tired from growing horns and getting scolded.

But when he laid his head on the pillow and closed

his eyes, sleep wouldn't come. His body felt tired, but his head was wide awake. His head was awake thinking Bad thoughts.

Thinking about things with horns. Thinking about long black marks that smelled smoky.

* * *

"Beep!"

Jasper sat up and looked around. It was the middle of the night. Mom and Dad were asleep in their bed. Ori was asleep in his bed across the alley and one house down. His Nan was asleep in her bed in her apartment that Jasper visited every Wednesday.

But Jasper was wide awake.

He got up and crept down the hall to his parents' room. In the dark he could just make out Dad on his side of the bed and Mom on hers. Even if he couldn't see them, he knew whose side of the bed was whose. One side was snoring.

The best way to get in was from the foot of the bed. He lifted the covers and pulled on the sheet until it untucked. Head first, he burrowed in without waking Mom or Dad. He popped out between them, sighed and closed his eyes.

So cozy. So safe. So —

"Beep!"

Jasper sat up. Mom and Dad did, too.

"Did you hear that?" Jasper asked them.

Chapter 4

In the morning when Dad woke him for school, Jasper was in his own bed. "My head hurts," he said.

"Maybe you're getting sick." Dad laid a hand on Jasper's forehead. Jasper put his hands over Dad's hand and pressed hard.

"Can I stay home from school?"

Dad said, "As long as you don't wake Mom. She had a bad sleep."

"Did she keep hearing a beep?" Jasper asked.

Dad looked at Jasper with raccoony eyes. "As

a matter of fact, she did. And so did I. You kept shouting it out. I'll leave her a note when I head out. You stay in bed until she wakes up."

Jasper let Dad take his hand away. His head didn't hurt as much now that Dad had pressed it, now that he could stay home from school.

He hardly ever got to stay home, even though Mom was always there. Mom worked at home. Dad went somewhere else to work. He took the bus, but Mom only took her mug of tea down the stairs to her office in the basement.

Whenever Jasper was allowed to stay home, the first thing he did was work on his lint collection. He'd scrape new lint off the dryer screen, then bring it back upstairs to sort it into the compartments of his lint box. He'd stick his nose right in the box and breathe that special flowery lint smell, the fabric-softener-clean-clothes-start-of-a-new-day smell that he loved. He could do this any day, but working on his lint collection in his pajamas when everybody else was at school doing math was the best.

Because he was supposed to stay in bed today until Mom got up, Jasper didn't scrape new lint off the dryer screen right away. He took his box off the shelf and carried it back to bed. He sniffed and poked at what he'd already collected. As he was sniffing and poking, he remembered the chip and candy machine and how all the treats were arranged inside it. The lint box was similar, with the different gray lint that he scraped off the dryer screen in their compartments, and the other kinds of lint in theirs.

And Jasper remembered the impatient *Beep!* the

machine had made. He remembered how he kept hearing it in his sleep and how, every time, it woke him up. Because of the beep, he felt so so so tired and his fingers so so so clumsy. So clumsy that, as he was working, the box of lint almost spilled all over the bed.

If Jasper stayed home from school today and worked on his lint collection, something Bad might happen. He might mix the colors of the lint he had worked so hard to sort. He might even do it on purpose! He might stand on the back porch and —

He shut his eyes tight, afraid to see the lint spilling over the railing and blowing away.

Now his head hurt even more from thinking Bad thoughts. He got out of bed and returned his lint box to the shelf.

In the kitchen, Dad was talking to the coffee maker. "Nice and strong and hot," he said.

"I changed my mind," Jasper said.

Dad turned to him. "Okay. I'll make you a sandwich. Get yourself an orange to have with your breakfast. And an apple for your lunch."

Jasper went to the fridge. Instead of opening the fruit drawer, he pushed all the yogurt containers aside. Maybe Mom had found the can of Torpedo High Energy Drink and poured it out.

It was still there. He looked back at Dad, then reached for the can and took a sip. Surprise! No little bombs went off in his mouth. It tasted different, sweeter and thicker, like syrup. He checked the can to see if it was the same drink. And now that he'd taken a sip, he wanted another. Today, he didn't have to scratch his tongue in between.

After four sips, he hid the can again. He grabbed an orange and an apple from the drawer and ran to the table — fast! He ate his cereal and his orange while bouncing on his chair. After he finished, he fitted the orange peel over his teeth and smiled at Dad across the table. "Look at me! I'd better go to the dentist! My teeth look so so so Bad."

Dad took a swig of his nice, strong, hot coffee. "Actually, Jasper. I have a headache, too."

Jasper spat the orange peel onto his plate. "Mine's gone! Now I have High Energy!"

Dad squeezed between his eyes with his fingers. He asked Jasper to get dressed.

Jasper ran to his room. Fast! He stripped off his pajama top — fast! — and flung it in the corner. He was supposed to put it in the laundry basket, but he didn't. He pulled on a shirt. Fast! He opened his underwear drawer. Fast!

In the drawer was a whole set of Day-of-the-Week underpants that his Nan had bought him. "What day is it?" Jasper shouted.

"Friday!" Dad shouted back. "Don't shout! Mom's sleeping!"

Jasper clawed through the drawer searching for *Friday*. Underpants from Nan reminded him of Nan's black mark expression. That reminded Jasper of his own smoky mark in the alley. And now that he had drunk the Bad drink again — on purpose! — he would probably get another black mark. People would walk through the alley and see two black marks, then look at Jasper's house and shiver, wondering who lived there.

He pulled out a pair of underpants. *Saturday*. Cackling, he stepped out of his pajama bottoms and into the *wrong* Day-of-the-Week underpants.

He felt so so so so Bad!

Chapter 5

At school, Ms. Tosh took attendance. She called out everybody's name.

"Ori?"

"Here!"

"Isabel?"

"Here!"

"Jasper?"

"Beep!" Jasper called out.

"Jasper's here!" Ori called.

While everyone else was doing the Calendar,

Jasper hid behind a book and practiced saying "Beep!" in the same impatient way the drink machine had. He squirmed and bounced on his chair. Margo, who sat next to him, leaned over. "Do you have ants in your pants?"

If she only knew about the *wrong* underpants! Jasper grinned at her, showing all his teeth. Still bouncing, he took out his pencil case and dug through it for an orange marker to color his white teeth.

Ms. Tosh tapped. That was what she always did when Jasper lost focus. She would come over to his desk and tap his worksheet. Jasper looked up and saw the math worksheet in front of him and Ms. Tosh standing over him, waiting with crossed arms for him to start.

The worksheet was hard. It was especially hard because while Ms. Tosh had been explaining what to do, Jasper had been hunched behind his book whispering "Beep!" and bouncing on his chair instead of paying attention.

Tom has 15 rabbits in a pen in his backyard. One day he forgets to close the pen, and 6 rabbits escape. How many are left?

All the other kids were doing the math. Some were counting on their fingers.

"Was Tom Bad?" Jasper asked Ms. Tosh.

"I don't think so. He didn't let the rabbits out on purpose."

Jasper hadn't bought the Torpedo High Energy Drink on purpose, but he had drunk it on purpose. The first time, Dad had said he could. But this morning Jasper hadn't asked permission because he knew what Dad would say if he was paying attention.

Dad would say, "No."

But Jasper had drunk it anyway!

Ms. Tosh explained that Jasper was supposed to use subtraction to figure out how many rabbits were left. "And you can draw pictures if you think that will help."

Pictures *would* help. Jasper turned over the worksheet where there was more room for rabbits.

He drew a line. It was so wiggly from Jasper's

bouncing that it could only be the rabbit's furry back. Jasper drew long, long ears and a short, puffy tail and long, long whiskers. When he sat back and looked at the drawing, he saw a rabbit with High Energy, jumping up and down so so so fast.

Except it hardly looked like a rabbit at all! Jasper scratched it out. Back and forth with the pencil in his fist, he scribbled over the Bad rabbit. Before he knew it, he'd drawn a black mark.

The bell rang for recess.

Uh-oh, Jasper thought. He needed answers — fast! — or he couldn't go out. In seconds, he filled in all the blanks, torpedoed to the front of the class and dropped his worksheet on Ms. Tosh's desk. Then he torpedoed outside with his friends, shivering from his Badness.

Every answer he'd written down was wrong!

For the whole recess, Jasper ran around the school. Ori trotted after him, trying to keep up. "Why are you running, Jasper?"

"I have High Energy," Jasper said, breathing hard. He told Ori about the Torpedo High Energy Drink. "I still have some. It's in the fridge at home. Come over after school and try it."

"I'm not allowed drinks like that," Ori said.

"Neither am I!" Jasper said, cackling and speeding off.

Chapter 6

Dad made Jasper go to bed early because of his Bad sleep the night before. Also because he had a soccer game in the morning. Jasper was so so so tired that he slept for twelve hours without even taking a break to dream. When he woke on Saturday morning, he felt good.

At breakfast, Dad told Jasper he only needed two things to be a star at soccer: a good sleep and a good breakfast.

"What about a ball?" Jasper asked.

"Three things, then. Good sleep? Check. Good breakfast? Check." Dad set two plates of bacon and eggs on the table. "With your good sleep and your good breakfast behind you, you'll feel confident and strong for the game, Jasper."

"My breakfast is in *front* of me," Jasper said.

"But after you eat it, it will be behind you."

"Won't it be *in* me?"

"*Eat*," Dad said, sitting down at the table.

Jasper ground a lot of pepper onto his egg. He liked so much pepper that his egg looked dirty. "What do you mean, 'confident'?" he asked.

"Sure of yourself," Dad said.

Jasper put down the pepper grinder and patted his head and body. He was sure it was him. "I'm confident," he said.

"Good. If you're confident, you won't be afraid of the ball."

"I'm not," Jasper said, picking up his dirty toast and egg and taking a bite.

"Good," Dad said. "That's what I like to hear."

Dad started eating his own bacon and egg breakfast. "I forgot your milk," he said.

"I'll get it."

Jasper pulled out a bottom drawer and stood on it so that he could reach the glasses in the cupboard. He poured himself some milk from the fridge.

"See?" Dad said. "You're getting your own milk now, not expecting me or Mom to get it for you. You must be feeling really confident. So, Jasper? When you're on the soccer field? When the ball comes to you? Pretend it's a big jug of milk. Run after it like you're thirsty."

Jasper looked at Dad. "Is there milk inside a soccer ball?"

"No," Dad said. "Of course not."

Jasper put the milk jug back in the fridge. The Torpedo High Energy Drink was still tucked in the back corner. He took it out and jiggled it. A lot was left — more than half. Jasper thought of the syrupy taste. He remembered how one sip was never enough.

He showed Dad the can. "If I had another drink of this, I'd feel so so so confident. I'd have High Energy."

"Then drink it," Dad said.

"All of it?" Jasper asked.

"Drink as much as you want."

In the bathroom, the hair dryer shut off. Jasper took a quick sip of the Bad drink. And another. He started running on the spot.

"That's it!" Dad said. "I can see you're really going to chase that ball today!"

Jasper had two more sips before Mom got to the kitchen. By then he was back at the table, bouncing on his chair.

"Hurry, hurry, you two," she said. "We'll get the lates."

Jasper gobbled his three pieces of bacon. Fast! He glugged his milk. Fast! Then he torpedoed to his bedroom to dress. He dug through his underwear drawer — fast! — until he found a pair of underpants that said *Wednesday*. Cackling, he put them on.

His soccer uniform was laid out on the bed — the sunny yellow shirt, the black shorts, the shin pads. The long black socks with the yellow stripes on the cuffs.

When Jasper finished dressing, he torpedoed to the tall mirror in the hall. Looking at his whole self in the mirror, at the black and yellow uniform with the yellow stripes under his knees, he said, "Buzz!"

He looked like a bee. But when he turned up the sock cuffs so the stripes didn't show, he just looked like a boy in a soccer uniform.

* * *

In the car on the way to the game, Mom said, "Jasper? Please don't kick the back of my seat."

"I'm running," Jasper told her. "I can't stop."

"Because he's so fired up for the game," Dad said.

"No," Jasper said. "It's because I'm Bad."

Mom swung around in her seat. "Jasper! You are *not* bad!"

"Yes, I am," he said.

"Maybe you're not the best on the team. But you're not bad," she said.

"I *am* Bad. I'm probably the Worst on the team," Jasper said.

"You're not!"

"Who's the Worst then?" Jasper asked.

Mom faced forward in her seat without answering.

"Mom?" Jasper asked, his legs running in the air, but not kicking Mom's seat. "Who's the Worst?"

"I have no idea," she said. "I only watch you play. I don't compare you with the other kids."

"So maybe I am the Worst," he said.

"It doesn't matter who's the best and who's the worst," she said. "What matters is that you play as well as you can and have fun."

"He's sure going to do that today, aren't you, Jasper?" Dad said, turning around in his seat to smile at Jasper. "Remember, the ball is a jug of milk. You're thirsty. Run after it! Run!"

"Fast!" Jasper shouted.

They were only a little bit late for the game. Coach Ben was giving his Hurray Talk to all the players. Jasper ran over and joined the circle.

"Hurray! Jasper's here!" Coach Ben said.

All the kids called out, "Hurray, Jasper!"

"Let's play our best today," Coach Ben said.

He put his big hand in the middle of the circle.

All the kids slapped their smaller hands on top of his. When there was a big pile of small hands in the middle, they shouted "Hurray!" one last time.

Except for Jasper. Today Jasper shouted, "Beep!"

Then Coach Ben threw all their hands in the air and everybody ran off, except Jasper. Coach Ben put his arm around him and held him back.

"I said 'beep' when everybody else said 'hurray,'" Jasper admitted to Coach Ben, who was leading him over to the big net bag of soccer balls.

Coach Ben fiddled with his cap brim. He coughed and picked up a ball. "Do you see this, Jasper?"

Jasper wondered if Coach Ben needed glasses. "It's a soccer ball."

"Can it hurt you?" Coach Ben asked.

"It could," Jasper said.

"But it's much more likely that you'll hurt the ball. Right, Jasper? Punch it. Go ahead."

"I thought I wasn't supposed to touch it with my hands," Jasper said.

"Go ahead. Punch it. Just this once."

Jasper punched the ball and laughed. "That's Bad!"

"It sure is! Now kick it." Coach Ben dropped the ball on the ground.

Jasper kicked the ball. It torpedoed all the way into the parking lot and bounced off somebody's car.

"Wow!" Coach Ben said.

"Was that Bad?" Jasper asked.

"That was terrific! Can you do that during the game?"

"Yes!" Jasper said.

"Good boy!" Coach Ben patted Jasper on the

shoulder. He called out to the other kids, "Positions, players! Get in position!"

Just as Jasper was about to run onto the field and take his position, Coach Ben noticed Jasper's socks. The cuffs were still turned up so that the stripes didn't show. "Just a second, Jasper." Coach Ben turned down Jasper's cuffs so the stripes showed again, the way he did before every game.

"Buzz!" Jasper said. "I'm a bee!"

"That's the stuff," Coach Ben said.

Jasper ran off buzzing.

The whistle blew and the ball came flying down the field toward Jasper. His High Energy made him run. Fast! In a second he was at the edge of the field where all the dandelions grew. It was like a dandelion garden there between the soccer field and the trees.

"Buzz, buzz, buzz!" Jasper sang as he kicked through the dandelions. He could see the yellow powder gathering on his black socks. This was what bees did. They played in the flowers collecting pollen on their legs. Then they took it back to the hive and made honey things with it. He'd learned it in school.

Jasper got an idea. He could be a Bad bee. A bee who beeped instead of buzzed! A bee who beeped and stung people!

Jasper burst back onto the field, beeping and zigzagging. He chased after the boy who had the ball, and when he got close enough he jabbed with his pointer finger stinger. "Beep!"

"Hey!" the boy said, grabbing his waist. "That tickles!"

"Beep! Beep!" Jasper said, stinging.

The boy buckled over, laughing.

Jasper thought the referee would blow his whistle for stinging, but he didn't. Somebody else got the ball so Jasper went after him.

"Look at him run!" he heard Dad call. "Go, Jasper! Go!"

The boy Jasper was chasing saw Jasper's stinger pointed right at him. His eyes got wide and he ran the other way. "Don't!" he cried, already laughing. "No tickling! No!"

"Beep!" Jasper said as somebody from Jasper's team kicked the ball and scored a goal.

At the break, Dad and Coach Ben rushed at Jasper, smiling because Jasper's team was winning. They'd never won a game before.

“Good work, Jasper!”

“But I was Bad,” Jasper said. “I was so so so so Bad. Didn’t you see me?”

Dad picked up Jasper and lifted him high in the air. When Jasper was back on the ground, Coach Ben patted him all over, like he was trying extra hard to be confident in him.

“What a great game, Jasper. This is the first time that you’ve stayed with the other kids. Usually, you’re over at the side of the field by yourself.”

“That’s where the dandelions are,” Jasper said.

“Get back out there and do just what you’re doing,” Coach Ben told him. Then he turned to Dad. “A jug of milk? I would never have thought of that.”

Chapter 7

On Sunday, Nan was coming over for supper. Jasper planned to show her the black mark against him in the alley. He didn't plan to drink the Bad drink again, but as soon as he thought of the black mark, he wanted the Bad drink. Then he couldn't stop himself from drinking it. He snuck five sips.

When Nan arrived, they went out. Jasper went fast! Nan went at her normal speed. Jasper had High Energy and Nan didn't.

The black mark was faded from cars driving over

it, but Jasper could still see it. He got down on his knees and sniffed it. Too bad the smoky smell was gone.

"My goodness," Nan said. "You must have done something terrible."

"I did so many terrible things!" Jasper said.

He told her about stinging everybody at soccer. He told her about wearing the *wrong* Day-of-the-Week underpants. He told her about writing the *wrong* answers on his math worksheet — on purpose!

"But why are you doing these Bad things, Jasper?" Nan asked. "You're the best boy I know."

Jasper stared at Nan. He didn't want to tell her about the Bad drink. And he didn't want not to be her best boy anymore.

"Is it because you're having fun?" Nan asked.

"Yes!" Jasper said. "That's why!"

"Have fun, Jasper John, but not *too* much."

He got back on his bike. With Nan watching the alley for cars, he rode up and down, up and down — fast! — making wind. Right in front of Nan, he squeezed his brakes so they made their scary cat-screech sound.

"Jasper!" Nan cried, and stepped back with a hand pressing her heart. "That's what I meant by too much fun."

Jasper laughed. He rode over to look at the mark. "Nan?" he said, smiling. "That one's for stinging kids at soccer. The next one's for wrong underpants!"

At supper, Jasper still had High Energy. He bounced on his chair while he ate. When Mom asked him why he was bouncing again, Jasper said, "Because it's fun!"

Mom told him to stop. Then Dad told him to stop. Jasper said he couldn't. Nan frowned.

"No more bouncing," Dad said. "If you want to bounce, eat in your room."

Jasper stomped off with his plate. "No fair!" he shouted back. "Then I don't get to have supper with Nan!"

He had to sit alone in his room, bouncing on the bed. It wasn't fun.

Later, Nan came to say good-bye. "Am I still your best boy?" he asked.

"You're my best boy no matter what."

But there were tidal waves at bath time again. And in bed that night, Bad thoughts crowded into Jasper's head — black marks and orange teeth and stains on his clothes. He kept hearing *Beep! Beep!* and knew it meant *"Hurry! Hurry!"*

All he wanted to do was go to sleep.

* * *

On Monday morning, Jasper's head hurt again and he had Low Energy from his Bad sleep. At school he couldn't focus on anything Ms. Tosh said.

Ori followed Jasper outside at recess. "You're not running today, Jasper."

Jasper was dragging his feet. He dragged himself over to the picnic table. "I need a little nap," he said, and he lay down on the table.

"Did you drink the Bad drink again, Jasper?" Ori asked.

"Yes." Jasper closed his eyes.

"You have to stop. You have to pour it out."

"I know," Jasper said. "I feel so so so Bad today. I never want to drink it again."

Ori leaned so close that Jasper could smell his breath. "The thing is, Jasper?"

Jasper opened his eyes. "What did you have for breakfast?"

"Cinnamon toast. Jasper, you have to stop drinking that Bad drink. You have to drink good things instead."

"I had a glass of milk at breakfast."

"Then you have to eat something good. Eat the most good food. The most good food will take away the Badness and make you good again."

"The most good food?" Jasper said. "You mean *celery*?"

After school, Mom was waiting to walk Jasper and Ori home. She always walked them home because

Ori's mom was busy with Ori's baby sister. Ori gave her the instructions.

"Jasper has to eat celery as soon as he gets home. I would come to help him eat it, but I have my violin lesson."

Jasper dragged his feet because he was so tired and because he didn't want to eat celery.

"Jasper hates celery," Mom said.

"I know, but it's good for him," Ori said. "Cut it into little pills. He should take it with milk. Or juice."

Mom laughed. "You sound like a doctor, Ori."

"The thing is, Jasper's my friend. I know what's good for him."

When they reached the alley where Ori turned to go home, he hugged Jasper. Jasper hugged him back. "You can do it, Jasper," Ori said.

"I guess you had a hard day," Mom said after Ori left.

Jasper groaned.

At home, Jasper sat at the kitchen table holding his headache in his hands. He didn't bounce on the chair. He couldn't. He had even Lower Energy than at school.

Mom cut the celery on the cutting board. She brought it to him on a plate with a glass of milk. Jasper looked at the pale green celery pills.

"What don't you like about celery?" Mom asked.

"The taste," Jasper said. "And how it has strings. I don't like food with strings."

"Just take one. With a big swig of milk. And if that goes all right, you can try another."

Jasper picked up one of the celery pills. He could feel the strings! Then he sniffed it. Strings!

“Go on,” Mom said. “One or two, then I’ll make you something you like. Or — here’s an idea. You can just *tell* Ori you ate some celery.”

“Mom!” Jasper said. “That’s lying!”

“Okay, okay. I’ll leave you to it. I have a phone call to make.”

Mom left Jasper in the kitchen, staring at the celery pills. He poked at them and pushed them around on his plate. Finally, he took a pill in one hand and the glass of milk in the other. He swigged the milk and, holding it in his mouth, jammed one of the celery pills between his lips.

BLAHHH!!!

Milk sprayed everywhere. Jasper coughed and gagged. He stomped over to the sink for a cloth. After he had wiped up the spit-milk, he went straight to the fridge to take out the Bad drink and pour it down the sink.

The can was behind even more yogurt containers full of furry green food. Jasper jiggled it to see how much was left. A little less than half.

And he got an idea. It would be so so so much easier to swallow a pill with Torpedo High Energy Drink than with milk.

Chapter 8

"Pour yourself a glass of milk," Dad told Jasper at breakfast on Tuesday morning.

"Can you pour it for me?" Jasper asked.

"I thought you were doing it yourself now. I'm busy making your lunch. Go ahead and pour it."

Jasper knew what would happen. If he opened the fridge, he wouldn't be able to stop himself from checking if the Torpedo High Energy Drink was still there. Then he wouldn't be able to stop himself from jiggling the can. He didn't want to drink it. He didn't like that Bad drink anymore. But he wouldn't be able to stop himself.

He went to the fridge and, just as he thought, ended up taking four sips of the Bad drink before he filled his milk glass. He torpedoed through breakfast, then torpedoed to his room to dress. When he opened his underwear drawer, he saw only one pair of Day-of-the-Week underpants.

"Mom!" he yelled. "Mom! Mom!"

Mom came to his room. "What, Jasper? What's wrong?"

"Where are all my underpants?"

"They're probably over in the corner where you keep throwing your dirty laundry." She pointed to the pile of clothes that had been growing and growing all week. "There are clean underpants in here, Jasper," she said, looking in his drawer.

"I can't wear those. I can only wear the Day-of-the-Week ones."

"Here," she said, fishing out a pair and holding them up. "This is exactly what you're looking for."

"Those say *Tuesday*!"

"Well, it is Tuesday," Mom said.

"That's what I mean," Jasper said.

Mom sighed. "Jasper, I'll do the laundry tonight. Now get dressed or you'll get the lates."

If he couldn't wear the *wrong* Day-of-the-Week underpants, the next best thing would be to wear the right underpants *inside out*! He put them on. Then, because his pants drawer was empty, Jasper went over to the pile of yesterday's clothes, put on *yesterday's* dirty jeans and cackled.

Dad called that it was time to go.

On the way to school, Jasper asked Dad, "Were you ever Bad when you were a kid?"

"You bet." Dad said this proudly, sticking out his chest.

"What did you do?"

"Once I said a Bad word to my mother."

"To Nan?" Jasper asked, and Dad nodded.

Jasper smiled, but really it made him feel watery inside to think of anybody saying a Bad word to Nan.

Dad told him about some other Bad things he'd done. He'd painted his brother's — Jasper's Uncle Tom's — toy soldiers with Nan's pink nail polish. He'd wrapped Uncle Tom's bike in toilet paper.

"Wow!" Jasper said.

"It was fun, but Tom was pretty mad. I'll tell you

what, Jasper. On the weekend, Mom is going out with her friends. It will be just you and me at home."

"Can we be Bad?" Jasper asked.

"That's just what I was thinking," Dad said.

And Jasper said, "Hurray!"

* * *

At school, they played What Am I? Ms. Tosh waited for all the kids to settle at their tables. Then she picked somebody to come to the front of the room. That person had to pretend to be something they'd learned about. Everybody else had to guess what it was.

Jasper's High Energy made it hard to focus again. He kept bouncing on his chair and wondering what Bad things he and Dad would do together on the weekend when Mom was out.

Zoë was at the front of the room flapping her hands and running in circles on the carpet. Everybody was shouting out.

"You're a bird!" Paul C. called.

Zoë shook her head and ran and flapped.

"You're the number eight!" Ori shouted.

"How could she be the number eight?" Leon asked.

"She's running in the shape of the number eight," Ori said.

Zoë changed the way she was running. She kept flapping.

How Bad would they be? Jasper wondered. He looked at Zoë. Why didn't she make a buzzing sound?

"She's a bee," Jasper said.

"Yes." Zoë ran flapping back to her table.

"Very good, Jasper," Ms. Tosh said. "It's your turn."

Now Jasper could focus! Everybody was looking at him!

Jasper got up from his table. He thought again about the walk to school with Dad. Dad had said a Bad word to Nan. Jasper could say a Bad word when he got to the front. That would be so so so so Bad!

Everybody was watching Jasper, who was dressed in inside-out underpants under yesterday's dirty jeans. He smiled back at everybody and stuck out his chest. They smiled, too, because he was walking so slowly, like there was glue on the floor. He was walking slowly to give himself time to think of the best Bad word.

One of his pant legs felt funny. Jasper stopped to shake his leg. That made everybody laugh. But soon they wouldn't be laughing. Soon they would be shocked at the sound of the Bad word exploding in the room. Which one? All of the best Bad words started with *B*.

"Jasper John Dooley," Ms. Tosh said, "we don't have all day."

Something was slipping down his pant leg. Jasper looked and saw it inching out around his ankle. Something white.

Something that looked a lot like underpants.

How? How had his underpants come off while he was wearing them? This had never happened before.

Jasper glanced back at the underpants left behind on the floor. He saw the word *Thursday*.

This morning he'd put on *Tuesday* underpants.

He kept walking, hoping nobody would notice. Nobody did. There were other things on the floor, like old crumpled worksheets and lunch boxes that should have been put away.

Once Jasper was standing in front of the class, he had to pretend to be something that nobody could guess so that everybody would keep looking at him. So that nobody would notice the *Thursday* underpants that had got stuck in the leg of yesterday's pants and were now lying on the classroom floor.

He began to wave his arms around and jump in the air. He did some twists and turns, like he was on a trampoline.

Everybody shouted out.

"You're a rabbit!"

"You're a spider!"

"You're a jumping bean!"

"If he was a jumping bean, he wouldn't wave his arms! Beans don't have arms."

He jumped and twisted and waved. After a lot of jumping and twisting and waving, he felt his High Energy turn to Low Energy. He still didn't know what he was.

"He's crazy!" somebody shouted.

Jasper flopped down on the floor and lay there panting.

Somebody else shouted, "He's dead!"

"Yes!" Jasper said.

He had died of embarrassment.

Chapter 9

After What Am I? they had to make good copies of the stories they'd written the day before. The *Thursday* underpants were still lying on the floor.

Jasper's story was about a boy who got the wrong drink out of a machine and drank it anyway. Horns grew out of his head. All he could think were Bad thoughts. He got lots of black marks that he wore in a necklace around his neck. The story ended before the underpants slid out of the boy's pant leg. Before the boy was so so sorry he had ever drunk the Bad drink. Before he died of embarrassment.

When Jasper finished the good copy of his Bad story, it was three pages long. He put up his hand and asked Ms. Tosh if he could get a paper clip from her desk. They used to staple their pages together until Jasper accidentally stapled his story to his stomach. Now stapling was Too Dangerous.

Ms. Tosh said, "Yes."

Really, Jasper wanted to get rid of the *Thursday* underpants. Any second the recess bell would ring and everybody would stand up from their tables. They might notice the underpants. Jasper flicked them with his foot on the way to the front. They landed part way under Isabel and Patty's table.

Now was the time to do something Bad. If he did something Bad now, everybody would look at him, not at the floor.

Jasper took the first page of his story and crumpled it into a ball. He did the same with the other two pages. He crumpled loudly so that Ms. Tosh would look up from her lesson book.

The bell rang.

"If you're finished your story, please leave it on my desk," Ms. Tosh told the class. She went over to the board and, turning her back, started writing.

Ori came up with his own neatly printed story just as — one, two, three — Jasper tossed his crumpled story balls onto Ms. Tosh's desk.

"Jasper! No!" Ori snatched up the balls. "You drank the Bad drink again, didn't you?" he whispered.

"The celery didn't work," Jasper said.

"Did you swallow it?"

"I couldn't!"

Ori hurried back to his table with the story balls. Jasper ran out of the room — fast! He stopped just outside the door, waiting for the room to empty so he could sneak back in and grab the underpants.

Ms. Tosh was still writing on the board. She wasn't ever going to leave. Ori had uncrumpled each of Jasper's story balls onto the seat of his chair. Now he sat on the wrinkly pages and bounced up and down to iron them out.

Ms. Tosh turned. "Ori? For goodness' sake! What are you doing?"

Jasper ran off.

* * *

Leon found the underpants after recess when he got up to sharpen his pencil.

"Yuck!" he said, holding them up. "Whose are these?"

Everybody screamed.

Jasper hid behind a book.

Leon waved the *Thursday* underpants in Isabel's face. "Are these yours?"

"No!" she shrieked. "Yuck!"

Leon shook them at Margo and Zoë. He shook them at Bernadette and Patty.

"They have to be a girl's. Only *girls* wear Day-of-the-Week underpants!"

Jasper popped up from behind his book when Leon said this. He felt his face turn so so so hot and red.

"Leon," Ms. Tosh said before he had waved the underpants in the face of every girl. "Bring those to the front right now."

Leon did. He skipped to the front waving the underpants like a tissue. Everybody yucked.

Jasper put up his hand and asked to go to the bathroom. Ms. Tosh said he could.

"Would you put these in the Lost and Found on the way?" Ms. Tosh asked.

Jasper stuffed the underpants in his pocket. Everybody laughed.

As soon as he left the classroom, he took out the

underpants again. Tears were spurting from his eyes. Mad tears. Embarrassed tears. He wiped his face with the *Thursday* underpants. He blew his nose.

Jasper was so so mad at that drink! So so mad and so so embarrassed. He muttered all the Bad *B* words he knew, but they didn't help.

Just ahead, two boys went into the bathroom. They looked like they were in Grade Six. All Jasper wanted was to take off the inside-out girls' underpants he was wearing. But he didn't want to take them off with two big Grade Six boys in the bathroom.

The girls' bathroom was beside the boys' bathroom. Jasper went in.

He was surprised. The girls' bathroom was almost the same as the boys' bathroom. It wasn't painted pink. He locked himself in a stall and took off his shoes so he could take off yesterday's pants. Then he took off the inside-out *Tuesday* underpants and put yesterday's pants back on. He was standing in sock feet with two pairs of underpants in his hands when he heard the bathroom door open and two girls come in, chatting.

"How did you do on the math test?" one asked in a squeaky voice.

"I don't want to talk about it," the other answered.

The lock on the stall rattled. Jasper jumped up on the edge of the toilet seat. He clung to the wall.

"Sorry," the squeaky girl said.

Jasper held his breath, balancing in his sock feet on the seat.

"Who's in there?" she asked.

Jasper kept quiet, and the two girls went into the other two stalls. Jasper heard two doors close.

"That's weird," the one girl squeaked. "If someone's in there, why doesn't she answer?"

"Look under the wall," the not-squeaky girl said.

"I'm looking. The weird thing is, I see shoes, but I don't see any feet."

"Maybe it's a ghost."

"Stop it. You're scaring me."

Sock feet on a toilet seat was almost the same as skates on ice. The same thing happened as the last time Jasper tried skating. He slipped. But when he slipped skating, he only fell on his bum. A so so so terrible thing didn't happen.

SPLOOSH!

"Did you hear that?" the squeaky one asked.

"I'm getting out of here," the other said.

Two toilets flushed. Jasper stood with one foot in the cold, yucky water, soaked to the ankle. Only when he heard the girls run out without washing their hands did he step out of the toilet. His wet sock slapped the floor. He picked up his shoes.

Down the hall to the office he trudged — step, slap, step, slap, step, slap — to tell the office assistant to call his mom. On the way he passed the Lost and Found box. He dropped the *Tuesday* and *Thursday* underpants in.

Chapter 10

"Why can't you put on your shoe?" Mom asked Jasper when she got to the school.

"I have *Toilet Foot*!!!"

"What's that?" She looked down at his foot in the sopping sock. "Oh."

"Let's go!"

Jasper and Mom left the school, Jasper's shoe foot stepping, his Toilet Foot slapping. Mom carried his shoe. "Can you tell me how this happened?"

Jasper said, "I don't want to talk about it!"

They walked the rest of the way without speaking. Step, slap. Step, slap. Step, slap.

At home, Jasper took a bath. Mom kept coming into the bathroom and smiling. Every time, Jasper put the wet cloth over his face. After she left, he added more hot water. He was going to stay in the bathtub for the rest of his life, even though his tummy was grumbling.

When Dad came home from work, Jasper was still there. Dad sat on the edge of the tub. "Let me see your foot."

Jasper lifted the good foot out of the water.

"Whoa! Wrinkly toes! Let me see the other."

Jasper shook his head.

"Please," Dad said, and Jasper lifted out the Toilet Foot.

"Same!" Dad said. "Wrinkly!"

Dad explained to Jasper why his toes got wrinkly in the bath. The toe skin filled up with bathwater until it was size Extra Large. The skin was Extra Large but the toes were Extra Small. No wonder the skin got all wrinkly.

"And you know what else?"

"What?" Jasper asked.

"The clean tub water has swished out both your feet, and the rest of you, inside and out."

"Really?"

Dad nodded. "Feel like coming out and having some supper?"

Jasper's tummy grumbled again. "What are we having?"

"Chicken, I think."

"Okay." Jasper climbed out of the tub and stood dripping on the mat, the cleanest he'd ever been in his life. Dad wrapped a towel around him.

Chapter 11

Before Mom went out on Saturday night, she looked in the fridge to make sure there was something for Jasper and Dad to eat. She opened a yogurt container and stuck her nose in.

"Yuck!"

Into the green bin went the furry green food. She looked in all the containers one by one and yucked. By the time she finished yucking, the fridge was almost empty.

"I guess we're ordering pizza," Dad said.

"Pizza! Hurray!" Jasper said.

Because the fridge was almost empty, Mom found the can of Torpedo High Energy Drink that had been tucked in the back. She held it away from her, like it might explode. "Where did *this* come from?"

Dad looked at the can. "I have no idea."

"These kinds of drinks are Bad," Mom told Jasper. "They're Very Dangerous for kids."

"I know that!" Jasper said.

Mom took the can to the sink. She was about to pour it out when Dad stopped her. "I'll drink it."

"Don't!" Jasper cried.

He rushed over, but it was too late! Dad tilted back his head and glugged down the rest of the Bad drink — fast! He squeezed the empty can so that it crumpled in his hand. Jasper shivered and backed away.

Mom frowned at Dad. "Didn't I just finish saying how Bad that drink is?"

He tossed the crumpled can in the recycling box and cackled.

"I've got to go," she said, shaking her head. "Have fun, you two."

Jasper followed Mom to the front door. "Do you have to go out?"

She put on her jacket. "I've been looking forward to tonight all week, Jasper. And so has your dad. He has some special things planned. Bye, sweetheart."

"Jasper!" Dad called from the kitchen. "Where are you? Let's get started!"

"Bye," Jasper said, hugging Mom hard, holding her tight until she pulled away.

He crept back to the kitchen and hovered in the doorway. "What's in that Bad drink, Dad?"

"The drink I just drank? A lot of sugar. A lot of caffeine."

"What's caffeine?"

"The same thing that's in coffee. Drinking that drink is like drinking ten cups of coffee. That's why it's not for kids."

Jasper felt better then. Mom and Dad drank coffee every morning. Dad waved the pizza menu and Jasper ran over.

"Okay. First things first," Dad said. "No vegetables."

"Hurray!" Jasper shouted.

"What kind of pizza do you want?"

"A Bad pizza!" Jasper said.

Dad read the menu. He found one called Dynamite Pizza, but it had peppers.

"Peppers are fruits but they seem like vegetables," Jasper said.

"Even if they *seem* like vegetables, we're not having them," Dad said.

"But tomato sauce is okay, right? A tomato is a fruit," Jasper said.

"Really?" Dad asked.

"Ms. Tosh said."

"If Ms. Tosh said, we can have it," Dad said.

They decided on the Meat Monster Pizza. While Dad was on the phone ordering, Jasper chanted in the background, "No veggies tonight! No veggies tonight! No celery especially!"

"Okay," Dad said, hanging up. "It'll be here in twenty minutes. That gives us just enough time to do another Bad thing."

"What?" Jasper asked.

"What's the Worst thing you could do at supper?" Dad asked Jasper.

Jasper thought about it. He thought hard and then he knew. "The worst thing you could do at supper is eat in your underpants."

Dad laughed and laughed. "That wasn't what I was thinking, but let's do it!"

"Hurray!" Jasper said. "Except let's wait for the pizza or you'll have to pay in your underpants."

"Jasper John," Dad said. "You astound me."

"What Bad thing were you thinking of?" Jasper asked.

"This!" Dad went to the freezer and took out a tub of ice cream.

"*Before* supper?" Jasper asked.

They looked at each other and cackled.

The pizza arrived just as they finished dessert. Dad paid in his pants. As soon as he closed the door, he let them fall to the floor, stepped out of them and left them lying in the hall. He brought the pizza to the kitchen in his checkered boxer shorts. Jasper dropped his pants on the kitchen floor.

"Mom would be so so so mad if we left our clothes all over the house," Jasper said.

"We're not going to do that, Jasper. We're going to stop being Bad and clean up before she gets home," Dad said.

"Okay," Jasper said. "What's the worst way to eat pizza?"

"I don't know — what?"

"Face down!" Jasper said.

Face down, the meat and cheese fell off. They ate it the normal way but didn't use napkins. After they finished, Dad asked, "Now what?"

"Now we lick the plates instead of rinsing them!"

It was easy to think of the next Bad thing to do. It was one of the Worst things they could do at their house.

Jump on the living room furniture!

Jasper raced Dad to the sofa and got there first. Dad threw some cushions on the floor and jumped on them.

"What about our digestion?" Jasper asked.

"What about it?" Dad replied.

Bad!

"Bad, Bad, Bad!" they chanted as they jumped. They got so hot jumping and chanting that Dad took off his shirt. Jasper took off his shirt, too.

Jasper got another Bad idea. "Let's say Bad words while we're jumping!"

"What Bad words?" Dad asked.

"Bad words that start with *B*! Like *bottom*!" Jasper shouted.

"Bottom!" Dad shouted.

"Bum!"

"Bum!"

"Butt!" they shouted at the same time.

Then both of them were jumping on the living room furniture, chanting, "Bottom! Bum! Butt!" — wearing only underpants! Nobody had ever done a so so so so Bad thing as that! At least not at Jasper's house.

While they were jumping and chanting, Jasper noticed a little flash of white in his dad's belly button. It was lint. That kind of lint — belly-button lint — was the rarest and hardest to find. The only place Jasper could get belly-button lint for his lint collection was from his dad's belly button.

Jasper took a huge leap from the sofa to the coffee table. From the coffee table, he planned to leap right onto the cushion Dad was jumping on. Then, before Dad knew it, Jasper would pluck the tiny bit of lint out of his belly button and run away with it. Dad would chase him, screaming "Stop, thief! Stop!" like he always did.

Except something Bad happened instead.

Something so so so so Bad.

When Jasper jumped from the sofa to the coffee table, the coffee table tipped and Jasper skidded down it and halfway across the living room carpet. When he finally stopped skidding, his head snapped back — *crack!* — against the edge of the coffee table.

"Ow!" Jasper roared. "Ow! Ow! Ow!"

Dad bent over him. "Jasper! Where does it hurt?"

"My leg!" Jasper shouted. "My leg!"

"Your leg?" Dad said. "Then why is there blood pouring from your head?"

Jasper could get up, but it hurt. His leg hurt. Dad said it wasn't broken because the hurt was on the outside. All down his leg, from his bottom to his calf, the skin was a bright, angry red.

Dad helped Jasper to the kitchen where he wet a towel to wipe the blood off. He put ice in a plastic bag and held it to Jasper's head while he tied Jasper's shirt around it.

"We're going to Emergency," he said.

First they had to find their pants. The worst thing for Jasper was getting his hurt leg in the pants. He started to cry.

"Ow! Ow! Ow!"

He limped out to the car.

"Ow! Ow! Ow!"

Dad drove away — fast! The tires squealed like an angry cat. "I'm really sorry, Jasper. I feel so bad about this."

"It's not your fault," Jasper said through his tears. "It was the drink."

"What drink?"

"The Bad drink you drank."

Dad said, "Hang in there, son. They'll fix you up. I love you so much, Jasper."

"I love you, too, Dad."

When they got to the hospital, Jasper limped slowly through the parking lot. He couldn't let Dad carry him because it would hurt too much if he touched his leg. The outside air felt cold on his bare chest. Only then did he remember he was wearing his shirt on his head. He probably looked so so funny, except that he was crying.

In Emergency, they talked to a nurse in a little booth. She had lots of nice smiles for Jasper, but none for Dad. Then he and Dad went over to wait with the other people who were having Emergencies. Dad sat, but Jasper stood because it hurt to bend his leg. Dad held his hand.

They called Jasper's name — fast!

Dad and Jasper followed another nurse into a little curtained room with bright white walls. The nurse gave Jasper a tissue to wipe his tears. "How did this happen, Jasper?"

"He was jumping on the —" Dad began.

"Sir?" the nurse said. "I'd like Jasper to tell the story."

She crossed her arms over her chest, the way Mom and Ms. Tosh sometimes did when they were mad. Dad shrank down. Jasper could tell he felt bad.

Jasper blew his nose. "After soccer practice I was so so so thirsty from being a bee that I got a drink from the machine, a Bad drink, but I drank it anyway even though it was the same as ten cups of coffee. Then so so so many Bad things happened that I don't want to talk about it. Me and Dad were only Bad because Dad drank the rest of the Bad drink and Mom went out so we jumped on the living room furniture in our underpants saying Bad words that start with *B*. It was fun until I tried to steal his belly-button lint and that's how this happened."

The nurse blinked at Jasper. She started to laugh. And Jasper laughed, too. The laughing erased all the crying he'd done.

"What Bad words?" she asked.

"Bottom! Bum! Butt!" Jasper said.

The nurse shook her head. "Bad!" Then she looked at Dad. "So your wife's out?"

“Yes,” Dad said.

Now she looked sorry for him instead of mad. She unwrapped Jasper’s head.

“Wow!” Jasper said when he saw all the blood on his shirt. “I should be dead!”

“A head bleeds a lot when it’s cut,” the nurse said. “But it’s stopped. Tell me if this hurts.”

“My leg hurts,” Jasper said.

“Well, your head is going to need stitches.”

“Stitches?” Jasper gasped.

The nurse said, “Stitches will make you look like a pirate. You’ll look *Bad*.”

“Hurray!” Jasper said.

The doctor who came to do the stitches was so nice. The pockets of her white coat were stuffed with suckers. She invited Jasper to take a sucker every time she did something that hurt. Nothing hurt too much. She peered and poked at his scalp. When she showed him the needle she was going to use to freeze his cut before she stitched him, she insisted he take a sucker.

"Uh-oh," Dad said.

Dad was holding Jasper's hand. At least that was what Jasper thought — except it turned out that, really, Jasper was holding Dad's hand.

Dad said, "I think I'm going to faint."

The doctor had to stop doctoring Jasper so she could help Dad over to the chair. She made him sit with his head between his knees.

"I'm sorry, Jasper," Dad said. "I'm not much help."

"Yes, you are," Jasper told him. "You drove the car."

The doctor stitched up Jasper's head. The freezing

needle pinched, then all he felt was a tugging on his scalp. She gave Jasper five more suckers, one for each stitch, bandaged him and showed Jasper her work in a mirror. The bandage went right around his head even though the cut was only at the back.

"I like it!" Jasper said. "You can look now, Dad."

Dad lifted his head out from between his knees. His face was as white as the doctor's coat.

The last thing the doctor did was check Jasper's leg. Slowly, Jasper stepped out of his pants. Up the side of his leg to the very edge of his underpants, the long red skid mark glowed.

“That,” the doctor said, “is maybe the worst rug burn I’ve ever seen.”

She gave Jasper some ointment and a lot more suckers. By then Dad could stand up. Slowly, he and Jasper limped out to the car, holding on to each other.

It was already dark. All the streetlights were on. “Mom should just be getting home now,” Dad said as they were driving away. From the way his shoulders slumped, Jasper could tell he was worried.

Jasper thought of the licked plates not put away and the tipped-over coffee table in the living room and all the cushions on the floor. He thought of the trail of blood to the kitchen. He leaned over and patted Dad’s shoulder.

“Dad? Just remember. We had so so so much fun!”

Chapter 12

Jasper couldn't go to soccer practice on Thursday because his rug burn still hurt. Also, he didn't want his bandage to come off while he was being a bee. He didn't really need the bandage anymore. He just liked the way it looked. Too bad it fell off the next day!

On Saturday morning, he was ready to play.

"Are you sure, Jasper?" Mom asked. "You're getting your stitches out this afternoon. Maybe you should wait."

"No, I'm ready now," he said.

"That's the stuff, Jasper!" Dad said. "Jump back in it."

"I think your uniform's in the wash," Mom said.

They went down to the basement together. Jasper wanted to scrape the lint off the dryer screen.

"Underpants," Mom said, pulling a plain pair from the dryer and handing them to him. "Oops. I forgot you like the Day-of-the Week ones. Here."

"Day-of-the-Week underpants are for girls," Jasper said. "Didn't you know that?"

"No," Mom said.

"I'm using my Day-of-the-Week underpants for something else now," Jasper said. He showed Mom. He put the laundry detergent lid in the underpants and pulled the waistband back like a slingshot. The lid fired across the room and hit the wall.

Mom jumped. "Just don't fire *at* anybody, okay? Shirt, shorts. Socks? Where are your socks?"

Jasper put on his shorts. He wrapped his shirt around his head because he wasn't wearing the bandage anymore. He fired the underpants slingshot a few more times.

"I can't find your socks anywhere, Jasper. Can you wear these for today?" She held up a pair of her own red knee socks. "You won't look the same as everybody else."

"That's okay," Jasper said. "I'm not the same as everybody else."

Because they were looking for Jasper's socks, they got the lates. The game had already started. Jasper ran straight onto the field in his red socks and scored a goal. Everybody was so surprised they stopped running and stared at Jasper.

And since everybody was just standing around, Jasper kicked the ball again and scored another goal.

Not once during the game did he go over to the side of the field where the dandelions grew. He really wanted to because a lot of them had turned into white puff balls. If he ran through them now, it would look like he was making smoke. But the red socks really wanted to play.

After the game all the kids crowded around Jasper, asking, "What happened to you, Jasper?"

"Why did I miss practice, you mean?"

He showed them the rug burn on his leg, which was still scabby. He showed them the stitches on the back of his head.

"Wow!" everybody said.

"I'm getting them out today. They pay you for it. They pay you in suckers."

"You play a lot better with stitches," one boy said.

"I want stitches!" another boy said.

"I'll tell you how to get them," Jasper said. "Do you see that drink machine over there? In front of the community center? Press C, then 3. But really? I wouldn't if I were you."

They went to the clinic instead of the Emergency Room to get the stitches out. The clinic didn't pay as much, just one sucker for the visit. Jasper was a little disappointed, but then it didn't hurt at all.

After they got home, Jasper and Ori rode bikes in the alley. They rode up and down, not too fast, only making a breeze. The black marks against Jasper were completely gone.

Jasper got an idea. Recycling day was coming up.

Some blue boxes were already out in the alley. They could make an obstacle course to ride around. He got off his bike and pulled the blue box away from the fence.

"Look!" Jasper called to Ori. "This is the drink I was telling you about."

He held up the half-crushed red and black can.

"Torpedo High Energy Drink," Ori read off the label. "Don't touch it, Jasper!"

The can was still buzzing with High Energy. Jasper could feel it vibrating in his hand. He could even hear it. He brought it close to his face so he could look inside and see if any of the Bad drink was left. A bee crawled out.

"AHHHHH!!!!"

Jasper dropped the can and ran. The bee chased him halfway down the alley, buzzing, buzzing and trying to sting him. It sounded so so so so mad!

Finally, it flew away.

"Wow!" Ori said, shaking his head. "You were drinking bees, Jasper! No wonder you felt Bad."

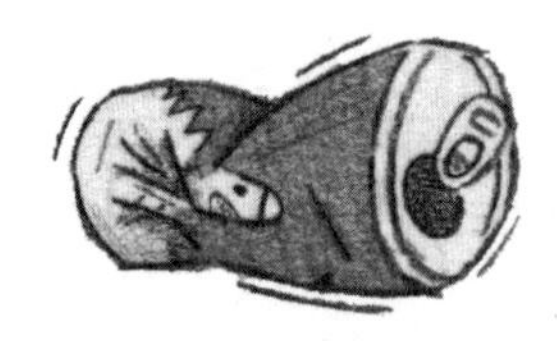

Praise for the Jasper John Dooley series

Jasper John Dooley: Star of the Week

★ Best Children's Books of the Year, Bank Street Children's Book Committee

"Well-written, funny, and engaging ... Share with kids looking for a boy version of Sara Pennypacker's Clementine series or with fans of Lenore Look's Alvin Ho books." — *Booklist*

"Readers will identify with many of Jasper's comical, age-appropriate issues." — *Kirkus Reviews*

"Readers will clamor for more from this unlikely but likeable and free-spirited hero." — *Reading Today,* International Reading Association

Jasper John Dooley: Left Behind

★ Named to *Kirkus Reviews'* Best Books of 2013

★ "So aptly, charmingly and amusingly depicted that it's impossible not to be both captivated and compelled." — *Kirkus Reviews,* starred review

"Emerging readers will enjoy following along with the quirky, charismatic boy and his friends and family in this humorous adventure." — *School Library Journal*

"A work of genius ... it has a playful sparkle that makes it truly exceptional." — *Toronto Star*

Jasper John Dooley: NOT in Love

★ "Adderson perfectly captures the trials of early childhood, and with brief text and a simple vocabulary, she breathes full life into her cast of characters." — *Kirkus Reviews,* starred review

★ "A triumph of its kind, suffused with refreshing, intelligent wackiness … This third volume confirms the series' exceptional subtlety and high literary quality." — *Quill and Quire,* starred review

"Caroline Adderson has nailed it. These kids walk, talk, scheme and worry just like their real-life counterparts — with lots of laughs along the way." — *Children's Book Review,* National Reading Campaign